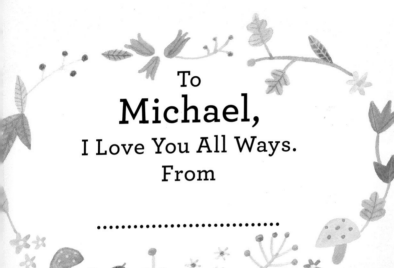

To
Michael,
I Love You All Ways.
From

....

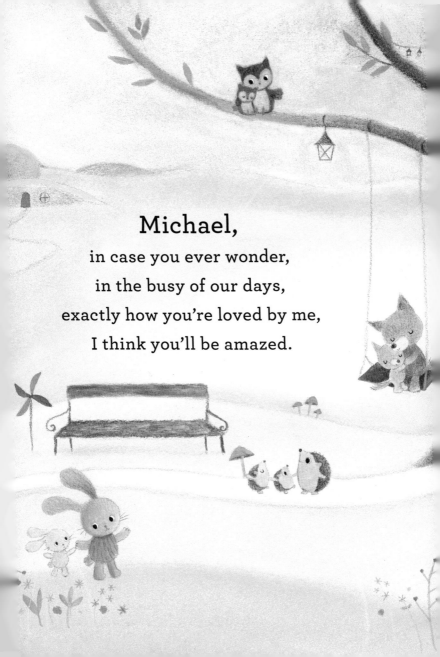

Michael,

in case you ever wonder,
in the busy of our days,
exactly how you're loved by me,
I think you'll be amazed.

Michael,

I love you first thing wide-awake

and nighttime sleepy too,

and every minute in between,
I love all the ways of you.

Michael,

I love you storytelling tales
to friends all gathered round

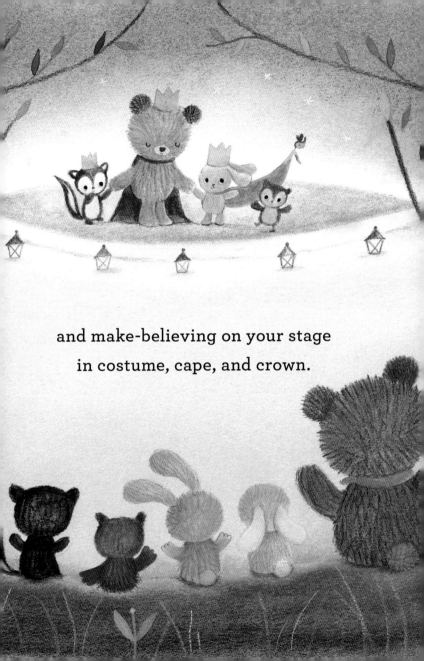

and make-believing on your stage
in costume, cape, and crown.

Michael,
I love you
underneath the sea

and side-by-side on land.

I love you
riding piggyback

and walking
hand-in-hand.

Michael,

I love you grumpy and upset,
excited, sassy, mad.

I love you cartwheel joyful

and under-blanket sad.

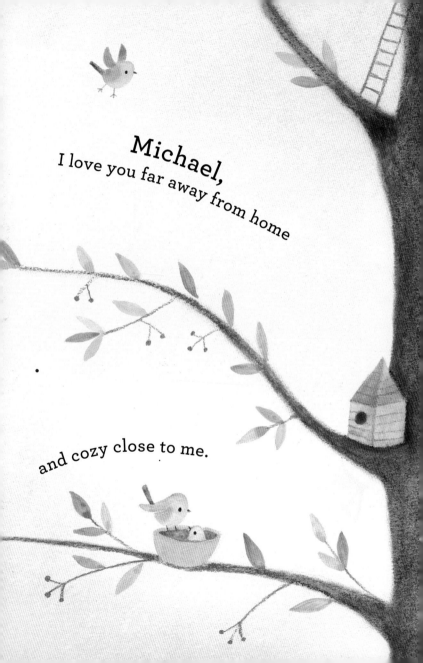

Michael,
I love you far away from home

and cozy close to me.

I love you quiet
in your thoughts

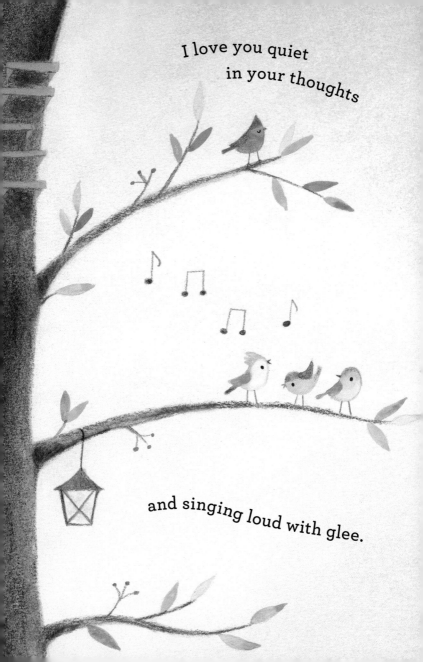

and singing loud with glee.

Michael,

I love you playing peekaboo
and swinging feet to sky.
I love you face up in the sun,
watching clouds go by.

Michael,

I love you covered

in the snow

and splashing

in the rain.

I love you mighty
mountain strong

and achy sick
with pain.

Michael,

I love you moody mischievous,
bending rules your way,

because my love is longer still
than any longest day.

Michael,

I love you at the age you are
and every year you grow

into more the special someone
I forever want to know.

Michael,

top to bottom, inside, through:
you're the certain of my days.

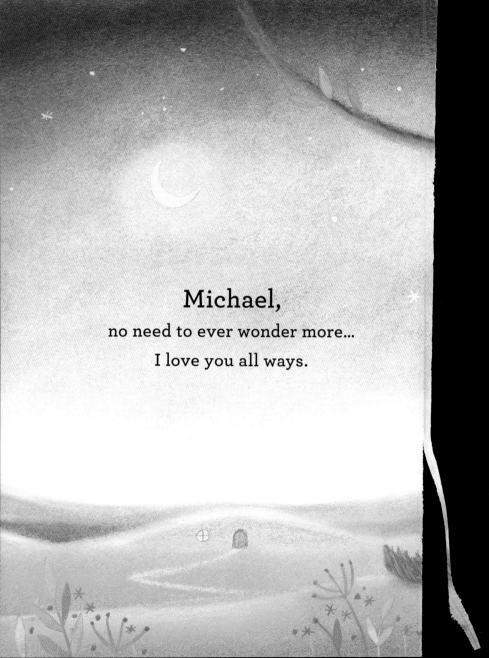

Michael,

no need to ever wonder more...

I love you all ways.

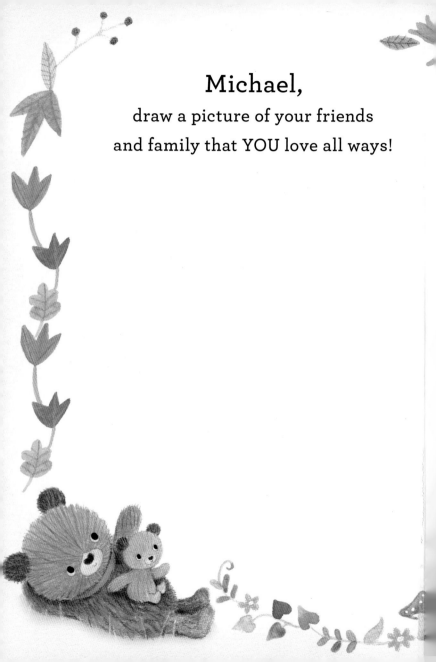

Michael,

draw a picture of your friends
and family that YOU love all ways!

Written by Marianne Richmond
Illustrated by Dubravka Kolanovic

Published by Put Me In The Story,
a publication of Sourcebooks.
P.O. Box 4410, Naperville, Illinois 60567-4410
(630) 536-1104
putmeinthestory.com

Date of Production: September 2022
Run Number: 5026919
Printed and bound in China (GD)
10 9 8 7 6 5 4 3 2 1

MIX
Paper from
responsible sources
FSC® C117745
www.fsc.org
FSC